The Sleeper and the Spindle

The Sleeper and the Spindle

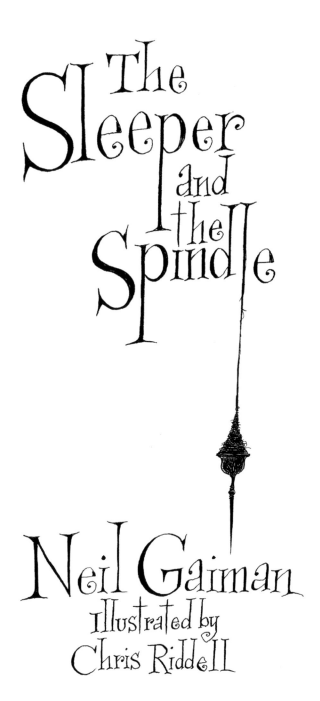

Neil Gaiman
Illustrated by Chris Riddell

BLOOMSBURY
LONDON   NEW DELHI   NEW YORK   SYDNEY

Bloomsbury Publishing, London, New Delhi, New York and Sydney

This story first appeared in *Rags & Bones: New Twists on Timeless Tales*,
published in 2013 by Little, Brown

This edition first published in Great Britain in October 2014 by Bloomsbury Publishing Plc
50 Bedford Square, London WC1B 3DP

www.bloomsbury.com
www.gaimanbooks.com

Bloomsbury is a registered trademark of Bloomsbury Publishing Plc

A CIP catalogue record for this book is available from the British Library

ISBN 978 1 4088 5964 3

Printed and bound in Italy by L.E.G.O. Spa

3 5 7 9 10 8 6 4 2

For Holly and Maddy, my daughters who woke me up
N.G.

For my daughter Katy, on the beginning of her quest
C.R.

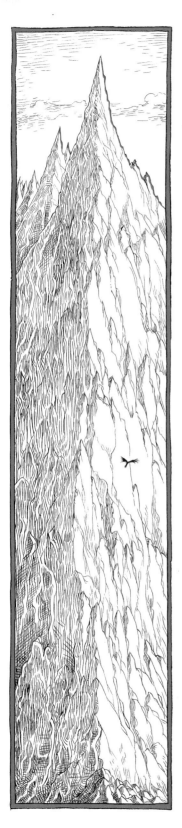

It was the closest kingdom to the queen's, as the crow flies, but not even the crows flew it. The high mountain range that served as the border between the two kingdoms discouraged crows as much as it discouraged people, and it was considered unpassable.

More than one enterprising merchant, on each side of the mountains, had commissioned folk to hunt for the mountain pass that would, if it were there, have made a rich man or woman of anyone who controlled it. The silks of Dorimar could have been in Kanselaire in weeks, in months, not years. But there was no such pass to be found, and so, although the two kingdoms shared a common border, nobody crossed from one kingdom to the next.

Even the dwarfs, who were tough, and hardy, and composed of magic as much as of flesh and blood, could not go over the mountain range.

This was not a problem for the dwarfs. They did not go over the mountain range. They went under it.

Three dwarfs, travelling as swiftly as one through the dark paths beneath the mountains:

"Hurry! Hurry!" said the dwarf at the rear. "We have to buy her the finest silken cloth in Dorimar. If we do not hurry, perhaps it will be sold, and we will be forced to buy her the second finest cloth."

"We know! We know!" said the dwarf at the front. "And we shall buy her a case to carry it back in, so it will remain perfectly clean and untouched by dust."

The dwarf in the middle said nothing. He was holding his stone tightly, not dropping it or losing it, and was concentrating on nothing else but this. The stone was a ruby, rough-hewn from the rock and the size of a hen's egg. It was worth a kingdom when cut and set, and would be easily exchanged for the finest silks of Dorimar.

It would not have occurred to the dwarfs to give the young queen anything they had dug themselves from beneath the earth. That would have been too easy, too routine. It's the distance that makes a gift magical, so the dwarfs believed.

The queen woke early that morning. "A week from today," she said aloud. "A week from today, I shall be married."

It seemed both unlikely and extremely final. She wondered how she would feel to be a married woman. It would be the end of her life, she decided, if life was a time of choices. In a week from now, she would have no choices. She would reign over her people. She would have children. Perhaps she would die in childbirth, perhaps she would die as an old woman, or in battle. But the path to her death, heartbeat by heartbeat, would be inevitable.

She could hear the carpenters in the meadows beneath the castle, building the seats that would allow her people to watch her marry. Each hammer blow sounded like a heartbeat.

Each hammer blow sounded like a heartbeat.

The three dwarfs scrambled out of a hole in the side of the riverbank, and clambered up into the meadow, one, two, three. They climbed to the top of a granite outcrop, stretched, kicked, jumped and stretched themselves once more. Then they sprinted north, towards the cluster of low buildings that made the village of Giff, and in particular to the village inn.

The innkeeper was their friend: they had brought him a bottle of Kanselaire wine – deep red, sweet and rich, and nothing like the sharp, pale wines of those parts – as they always did. He would feed them, and send them on their way, and advise them.

The innkeeper, chest as huge as his barrels, beard as bushy and as orange as a fox's brush, was in the taproom. It was early in the morning, and on the dwarfs' previous visits at that time of day the room had been empty, but now there must have been thirty people in that place, and not one of them looked happy.

The dwarfs, who had expected to sidle in to an empty taproom, found all eyes upon them.

"Goodmaster Foxen," said the tallest dwarf to the innkeeper.

"Lads," said the innkeeper, who thought that the dwarfs were boys, for all that they were four, perhaps five times his age, "I know you travel the mountain passes. We need to get out of here."

"What's happening?" said the smallest of the dwarfs.

"Sleep!" said the sot by the window.

"Plague!" said a finely dressed woman.

"Doom!" exclaimed a tinker, his saucepans rattling as he spoke. "Doom is coming!"

"We travel to the capital," said the tallest dwarf, who was no bigger than a child. "Is there plague in the capital?"

"It is not plague," said the sot by the window, whose beard was long and grey, and stained yellow with beer and wine. "It is sleep, I tell you."

"How can sleep be a plague?" asked the smallest dwarf, who was beardless.

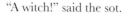

"A witch!" said the sot.

"A bad fairy," corrected a fat-faced man.

"She was an enchantress, as I heard it," interposed the pot-girl.

"Whatever she was," said the sot, "she was not invited to a birthing celebration."

"That's all tosh," said the tinker. "She would have cursed the princess whether she'd been invited to the naming-day party or not. She was one of those forest witches, driven to the margins a thousand years ago, and a bad lot. She cursed the babe at birth, such that when the girl was eighteen she would prick her finger and sleep forever."

The fat-faced man wiped his forehead. He was sweating, although it was not warm. "As I heard it, she was going to die, but another fairy, a good one this time, commuted her magical death sentence to one of sleep. Magical sleep," he added.

"So," said the sot. "She pricked her finger on something-or-other. And she fell asleep. And the other people in the castle – the lord and the lady, the butcher, baker, milkmaid, lady-in-waiting – all of them slept, as she slept. None of them has aged a day since they closed their eyes."

"There were roses," said the pot-girl. "Roses that grew up around the castle. And the forest grew thicker, until it became impassible. This was, what, a hundred years ago?"

"Sixty. Perhaps eighty," said a woman who had not spoken until now. "I know, because my Aunt Letitia remembered it happening, when she was a girl, and she was no more than seventy when she died of the bloody flux, and that was only five years ago come Summer's End."

". . . And brave men," continued the pot-girl. "Aye, and brave women too, they say, have attempted to travel to the Forest of Acaire, to the castle at its heart, to wake the princess, and, in waking her, to wake all the sleepers, but each and every one of those heroes ended their lives lost in the forest, murdered by bandits, or impaled upon the thorns of the rose bushes that encircle the castle –"

"Wake her how?" asked the middle-sized dwarf, hand still clutching his rock, for he thought in essentials.

"The usual method," said the pot-girl, and she blushed. "Or so the tales have it."

"Right," said the tallest dwarf. "So, bowl of cold water poured on the face and a cry of 'Wakey! Wakey!'?"

"A kiss," said the sot. "But nobody has ever got that close. They've been trying for sixty years or more. They say the witch –"

"Fairy," said the fat man.

"Enchantress," corrected the pot-girl.

"Whatever she is," said the sot. "She's still there. That's what they say. If you get that close. If you make it through the roses, she'll be waiting for you. She's old as the hills, evil as a snake, all malevolence and magic and death."

16

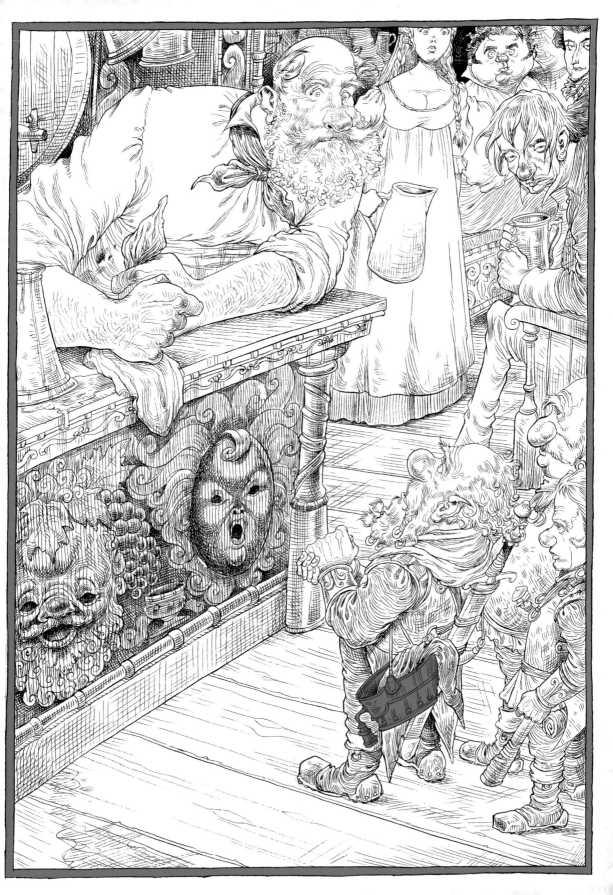

The smallest dwarf tipped his head on one side. "So, there's a sleeping woman in a castle, and perhaps a witch or fairy there with her. Why is there also a plague?"

"Over the last year," said the fat-faced man. "It started in the north, beyond the capital. I heard about it first from travellers coming from Stede, which is near the Forest of Acaire."

"People fell asleep in the towns," said the pot-girl.

"Lots of people fall asleep," said the tallest dwarf. Dwarfs sleep rarely: twice a year at most, for several weeks at a time, but he had slept enough in his long lifetime that he did not regard sleep as anything special or unusual.

"They fall asleep whatever they are doing, and they do not wake up," said the sot. "Look at us. We fled the towns to come here. We have brothers and sisters, wives and children, sleeping now in their houses or cowsheds, at their workbenches. All of us."

"It is moving faster and faster," said the thin, red-haired woman who had not spoken previously. "Now it covers a mile, perhaps two miles, each day."

"It will be here tomorrow," said the sot, and he drained his flagon, gestured to the innkeeper to fill it once more. "There is nowhere for us to go to escape it. Tomorrow, everything here will be asleep. Some of us have resolved to escape into drunkenness before the sleep takes us."

"What is there to be afraid of in sleep?" asked the smallest dwarf. "It's just sleep. We all do it."

"Go and look," said the sot. He threw back his head, and drank as much as he could from his flagon. Then he looked back at them, with eyes unfocused, as if he were surprised to still see them there. "Well, go on. Go and look for yourselves." He swallowed the remaining drink, then he lay his head upon the table.

They went and looked.

"Asleep?" asked the queen. "Explain yourselves. How so, asleep?"

The dwarf stood upon the table so he could look her in the eye. "Asleep," he repeated. "Sometimes crumpled upon the ground. Sometimes standing. They sleep in their smithies, at their awls, on milking stools. The animals sleep in the fields. Birds too, slept, and we saw them in trees or dead and broken in fields where they had fallen from the sky."

The queen wore a wedding gown, whiter than the snow. Around her, attendants, maids of honour, dressmakers and milliners clustered and fussed.

"And why did you three also not fall asleep?"

The dwarf shrugged. He had a russet-brown beard that had always made the queen think of an angry hedgehog attached to the lower portion of his face. "Dwarfs are magical things. This sleep is a magical thing also. I felt sleepy, mind."

"And then?"

She was the queen, and she was questioning him as if they were alone. Her attendants began removing her gown, taking it away, folding and wrapping it, so the final laces and ribbons could be attached to it, so it would be perfect.

Tomorrow was the queen's wedding day. Everything needed to be perfect.

"By the time we returned to Foxen's Inn they were all asleep, every man jack-and-jill of them. It is expanding, the zone of the spell, a few miles every day."

The mountains that separated the two lands were impossibly high, but not wide. The queen could count the miles. She pushed one pale hand through her raven-black hair, and she looked most serious.

"What do you think, then?" she asked the dwarf. "If I went there. Would I sleep, as they did?"

He scratched his arse, unselfconsciously. "You slept for a year," he said. "And then you woke again, none the worse for it. If any of you big people can stay awake there, it's you."

20

Outside, the townsfolk were hanging bunting in the streets and decorating their doors and windows with white flowers. Silverware had been polished and protesting children had been forced into tubs of lukewarm water (the oldest child got the first dunk and the hottest water) and scrubbed with rough flannels until their faces were raw and red. They were then ducked under the water, and the backs of their ears were washed as well.

"I am afraid," said the queen, "that there will be no wedding tomorrow."

She called for a map of the kingdom, identified the villages closest to the mountains, sent messengers to tell the inhabitants to evacuate to the coast or risk royal displeasure.

She called for her first minister and informed him that he would be responsible for the kingdom in her absence, and that he should do his best neither to lose it nor to break it.

She called for her fiancé and told him not to take on so, and that they would still be married, even if he was but a prince and she a queen, and she chucked him beneath his pretty chin and kissed him until he smiled.

She called for her mail shirt.

She called for her sword.

She called for provisions, and for her horse, and then she rode out of the palace, towards the east.

and then she rode out of the palace, towards the east.

It was a full day's ride before she saw, ghostly and distant, like clouds against the sky, the shape of the mountains that bordered the edge of her kingdom.

The dwarfs were waiting for her, at the last inn in the foothills of the mountains, and they led her down deep into the tunnels, the way that the dwarfs travel. She had lived with them, when she was little more than a child, and she was not afraid.

The dwarfs did not speak as they walked the deep paths, except, on more than one occasion, to say, "Mind your head."

"Have you noticed," asked the shortest of the dwarfs, "something unusual?" They had names, the dwarfs, but human beings were not permitted to know what they were, such things being sacred.

The queen had a name, but nowadays people only ever called her Your Majesty. Names are in short supply in this telling.

Names are in short supply in this telling.

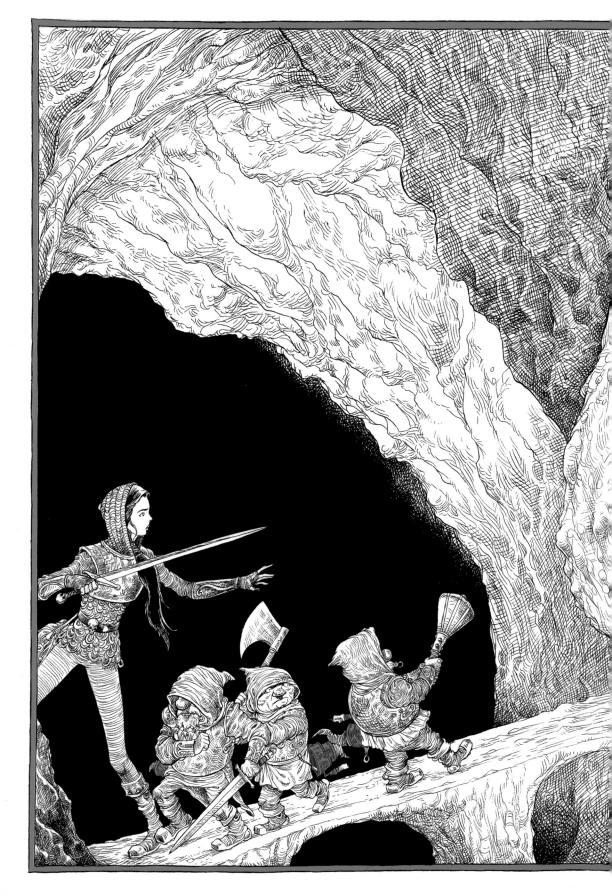

"I have noticed many unusual things," said the tallest of the dwarfs.

They were in Goodmaster Foxen's inn.

"Have you noticed, that even amongst all the sleepers, there is something that does not sleep?"

"I have not," said the second tallest, scratching his beard. "For each of them is just as we left him or her. Head down, drowsing, scarcely breathing enough to disturb the cobwebs that now festoon them . . ."

"The cobweb spinners do not sleep," said the tallest dwarf.

It was the truth. Industrious spiders had threaded their webs from finger to face, from beard to table. There was a modest web between the deep cleavage of the pot-girl's breasts. There was a thick cobweb that stained the sot's beard grey. The webs shook and swayed in the draught of air from the open door.

"I wonder," said one of the dwarfs, "whether they will starve and die, or whether there is some magical source of energy that gives them the ability to sleep for a long time."

"I would presume the latter," said the queen. "If, as you say, the original spell was cast by a witch, seventy years ago, and those who were there sleep even now, like Red-Beard beneath his hill, then obviously they have not starved or aged or died."

The dwarfs nodded. "You are very wise," said a dwarf. "You always were wise."

The queen made a sound of horror and of surprise.

"That man," she said, pointing. "He looked at me."

It was the fat-faced man. He had moved slowly, tearing the webbing, moved his face so that he was facing her. He had looked at her, yes, but he had not opened his eyes.

"People move in their sleep," said the smallest dwarf.

"Yes," said the queen. "They do. But not like that. That was too slow, too stretched, too *meant*."

"Or perhaps you imagined it," said a dwarf.

The rest of the sleeping heads in that place moved slowly, in a stretched way, as if they meant to move. Now each of them was facing the queen.

"You did not imagine it," said the same dwarf. He was the one with the red-brown beard. "But they are only looking at you with their eyes closed. That is not a bad thing."

The lips of the sleepers moved in unison. No voice, only the whisper of breath through sleeping lips.

"Did they just say what I thought they said?" asked the shortest dwarf.

"They said, 'Mama. It is my birthday,'" said the queen, and she shivered.

They rode no horses. The horses they passed all slept, standing in fields, and could not be woken.

The queen walked fast. The dwarfs walked twice as fast as she did, in order to keep up.

The queen found herself yawning.

"Bend over, towards me," said the tallest dwarf. She did so. The dwarf slapped her around the face. "Best to stay awake," he said, cheerfully.

"I only yawned," said the queen.

"How long, do you think, to the castle?" asked the smallest dwarf.

"If I remember my tales and my maps correctly," said the queen, "the Forest of Acaire is about seventy miles from here. Three days' march." And then she said, "I will need to sleep tonight. I cannot walk for another three days."

"Sleep, then," said the dwarfs. "We will wake you at sunrise."

She went to sleep that night in a hayrick, in a meadow, with the dwarfs around her, wondering if she would ever wake to see another morning.

he castle in the Forest of Acaire was a grey, blocky thing, all grown over with
climbing roses. They tumbled down into the moat and grew almost as high
as the tallest tower. Each year the roses grew out further: close to the stone of
the castle there were only dead, brown stems and creepers, with old thorns sharp as
knives. Fifteen feet away, the plants were green and the blossoming roses grew thickly.
The climbing roses, living and dead, were a brown skeleton, splashed with colour that
rendered the grey fastness less precise.

The trees in the Forest of Acaire were pressed thickly together, and the forest floor was
dark. A century before, it had been a forest only in name: it had been hunting lands, a royal
park, home to deer and wild boar and birds beyond counting. Now, the forest was a dense
tangle, and the old paths through it were overgrown and forgotten.

The fair-haired girl in the high tower slept.

All the people in the castle slept. Each of them was fast asleep, excepting only one.

The woman's hair was grey, streaked with white, and so sparse her scalp showed. She hobbled, angrily, through the castle, leaning on her stick, as if she were driven only by hatred, slamming doors, talking to herself as she walked. "Up the blooming stairs and past the blooming cook and what are you cooking now, eh, great lard-arse, nothing in your pots and pans but dust and more dust, and all you ever do is snore."

Into the kitchen garden, neatly tended. The old woman picked rampion and rocket.

Eighty years before, the palace had held five hundred chickens; the pigeon coop had been home to hundreds of fat, white doves; rabbits had run, white-tailed, across the greenery of the grass square inside the castle walls, while fish had swum in the moat and the pond: carp and trout and perch. There remained only three chickens. All the sleeping fish had been netted and carried out of the water. There were no more rabbits, no more doves.

She had killed her first horse sixty years back, and eaten as much of it as she could before the flesh went rainbow-coloured and the carcass began to stink and crawl with blueflies and maggots. Now she only butchered the larger mammals in midwinter, when nothing rotted and she could hack and sear frozen chunks of the animal's corpse until the spring thaw.

The old woman passed a mother, asleep, with a baby dozing at her breast. She dusted them, absently, as she passed and made certain that the baby's sleepy mouth remained on the nipple.

She ate her meal in silence.

She ate her meal in Silence.

It was the first great, grand city they had come to. The city gates were high and impregnable thick, but they were open wide.

The three dwarfs were all for going around it, for they were uncomfortable in cities, distrusted houses and streets as unnatural things, but they followed their queen.

Once in the city, the sheer numbers of people made them uncomfortable. There were sleeping riders on sleeping horses; sleeping cabmen up on still carriages that held sleeping passengers; sleeping children clutching their balls and hoops and the whips for their spinning tops; sleeping flower women at their stalls of brown, rotten, dried flowers; even sleeping fishmongers beside their marble slabs. The slabs were covered with the remains of stinking fish, and they were crawling with maggots. The rustle and movement of the maggots was the only movement and noise the queen and the dwarfs encountered.

"We should not be here," grumbled the dwarf with the angry brown beard.

"This road is more direct than any other road we could follow," said the queen. "Also, it leads to the bridge. The other roads would force us to ford the river."

The queen's temper was equable. She went to sleep at night, and she woke in the morning, and the sleeping sickness had not touched her.

The maggots' rustlings, and, from time to time, the gentle snores and shifts of the sleepers, were all that they heard as they made their way through the city. And then a small child, asleep on a step, said, loudly and clearly, "Are you spinning? Can I see?"

"Did you hear that?" asked the queen.

The tallest dwarf said only, "Look! The sleepers are waking!"

He was wrong. They were not waking.

The sleepers were standing, however. They were pushing themselves slowly to their feet, and taking hesitant, awkward, sleeping steps. They were sleepwalkers, trailing gauze cobwebs behind them. Always, there were cobwebs being spun.

"How many people, human people I mean, live in a city?" asked the smallest dwarf.

"It varies," said the queen. "In our kingdom, no more than twenty, perhaps thirty thousand people. This seems bigger than our cities. I would think fifty thousand people. Or more. Why?"

"Because," said the dwarf, "they appear to all be coming after us."

Sleeping people are not fast. They stumble, they stagger; they move like children wading through rivers of treacle, like old people whose feet are weighed down by thick, wet mud.

The sleepers moved towards the dwarfs and the queen. They were easy for the dwarfs to outrun, easy for the queen to outwalk. And yet, and yet, there were so many of them. Each street they came to was filled with sleepers, cobweb-shrouded, eyes tight closed or eyes open and rolled back in their heads showing only the whites, all of them shuffling sleepily forwards.

The queen turned and ran down an alleyway and the dwarfs ran with her.

"This is not honourable," said a dwarf. "We should stay and fight."

"There is no honour," gasped the queen, "in fighting an opponent who has no idea that you are even there. No honour in fighting someone who is dreaming of fishing or of gardens or of long-dead lovers."

"What would they do if they caught us?" asked the dwarf beside her.

"Do you wish to find out?" asked the queen.

"No," admitted the dwarf.

They ran, and they ran, and they did not stop from running until they had left the city by the far gates, and had crossed the bridge that spanned the river.

The old woman had not climbed the tallest tower in a dozen years. It was a laborious climb, and each step took its toll on her knees and on her hips. She walked up the curving stone stairwell; each small, shuffling step she took in agony. There were no railings there, nothing to make the steep steps easier. She leaned on her stick, sometimes, and then she kept climbing.

35

She used the stick on the webs, too: thick cobwebs hung and covered the stairs, and the old woman shook her stick at them, pulling the webs apart, leaving spiders scurrying for the walls.

The climb was long and arduous, but eventually she reached the tower room.

There was nothing in the room but a spindle and a stool, beside one slitted window, and a bed in the centre of the round room. The bed was opulent: crimson and gold cloth was visible beneath the dusty netting that covered it and protected its sleeping occupant from the world.

The spindle sat on the ground, beside the stool, where it had fallen seventy years before.

The old woman pushed at the netting with her stick, and dust filled the air. She stared at the sleeper on the bed.

The girl's hair was the golden yellow of meadow flowers. Her lips were the pink of the roses that climbed the palace walls. She had not seen daylight in a long time, but her skin was creamy, neither pallid nor unhealthy.

Her chest rose and fell, almost imperceptibly, in the semi-darkness.

The old woman reached down, and picked up the spindle. She said, aloud, "If I drove this spindle through your heart, then you'd not be so pretty-pretty, would you? Eh? Would you?"

She walked towards the sleeping girl in the dusty white dress. Then she lowered her hand. "No. I cannot. I wish to all the gods I could."

All of her senses were fading with age, but she thought she heard voices from the forest. Long ago she had seen them come, the princes and the heroes, watched them perish, impaled upon the thorns of the roses, but it had been a long time since anyone, hero or otherwise, had reached as far as the castle.

"Eh," she said aloud, as she said so much aloud, for who was to hear her? "Even if they come, they'll die screaming on the thorns. There's nothing they can do. That anyone can do. Nothing at all."

A woodcutter, asleep by the bole of a tree half-felled half a century before, and now grown into an arch, opened his mouth as the queen and the dwarfs passed and said, "My! What an unusual naming-day present that must have been!"

Three bandits, asleep in the middle of what remained of the trail, their limbs crooked as if they had fallen asleep while hiding in a tree above and had tumbled, without waking, to the ground below, said, in unison, without waking, "Will you bring me roses?"

One of them, a huge man, fat as a bear in autumn, seized the queen's ankle as she came close to him. The smallest dwarf did not even hesitate: he lopped the hand off with his hand-axe, and the queen pulled the man's fingers away, one by one, until the hand fell on the leaf mould.

"Bring me roses," said the three bandits as they slept, with one voice, while the blood oozed indolently on to the ground from the stump of the fat man's arm. "I would be so happy if only you would bring me roses."

They felt the castle long before they saw it, felt it as a wave of sleep that pushed them away. If they walked towards it their heads fogged, their minds frayed, their spirits fell, their thoughts clouded. The moment they turned away they woke up into the world, felt brighter, saner, wiser.

The queen and the dwarfs pushed deeper into the mental fog.

Sometimes a dwarf would yawn and stumble. Each time the other dwarfs would take him by the arms and march him forwards, struggling and muttering, until his mind returned.

The queen stayed awake, although the forest was filled with people she knew could not be there. They walked beside her on the path. Sometimes they spoke to her.

"Let us now discuss how diplomacy is affected by matters of natural philosophy," said her father.

"My sisters ruled the world," said her stepmother, dragging her iron shoes along the forest path. They glowed a dull orange, yet none of the dry leaves burned where the shoes touched them. "The mortal folk rose up against us, they cast us down. And so we waited, in crevices, in places they do not see us. And now, they adore me. Even you, my stepdaughter. Even you adore me."

"You are so beautiful," said her mother, who had died so very long ago. "Like a crimson rose in the fallen snow."

41

ometimes wolves ran beside them, pounding dust and leaves up from the forest floor, although the passage of the wolves did not disturb the huge cobwebs that hung like veils across the path. Also, sometimes the wolves ran through the trunks of trees and off into the darkness.

The queen liked the wolves, and was sad when one of the dwarfs began shouting, saying that the spiders were bigger than pigs, and the wolves vanished from her head and from the world. (It was not so. They were only spiders, of a regular size, used to spinning their webs undisturbed by time and by travellers.)

he drawbridge across the moat was down, and they crossed it, although everything seemed to be pushing them away. They could not enter the castle, however: thick thorns filled the gateway, and fresh growth was covered with roses.

The queen saw the remains of men in the thorns: skeletons in armour and skeletons unarmoured. Some of the skeletons were high on the sides of the castle, and the queen wondered if they had climbed up, seeking an entry, and died there, or if they had died on the ground, and been carried upwards as the roses grew.

She came to no conclusions. Either way was possible.

And then her world was warm and comfortable, and she became certain that closing her eyes for only a handful of moments would not be harmful. Who would mind?

"Help me," croaked the queen.

The dwarf with the brown beard pulled a thorn from the rose bush nearest to him, and jabbed it hard into the queen's thumb, and pulled it out again. A drop of deep blood dripped on to the flagstones of the gateway.

"Ow!" said the queen. And then, "Thank you!"

They stared at the thick barrier of thorns, the dwarfs and the queen. She reached out and picked a rose from the thorn-creeper nearest her, and bound it into her hair.

"We could tunnel our way in," said the dwarfs. "Go under the moat and into the foundations and up. Only take us a couple of days."

The queen pondered. Her thumb hurt, and she was pleased her thumb hurt. She said, "This began here eighty or so years ago. It began slowly. It only spread recently. It is spreading faster and faster. We do not know if the sleepers can ever wake. We do not know anything, save that we may not actually have another two days."

She eyed the dense tangle of thorns, living and dead, decades of dried, dead plants, their thorns as sharp in death as ever they were when alive. She walked along the wall until she reached a skeleton, and she pulled the rotted cloth from its shoulders, and felt it as she did so. It was dry, yes. It would make good kindling.

"Who has the tinder box?" she asked.

The old thorns burned so hot and so fast. In fifteen minutes orange flames snaked upwards: they seemed, for a moment, to engulf the building, and then they were gone, leaving just blackened stone. The remaining thorns, those strong enough to have withstood the heat, were easily cut through by the queen's sword, and were hauled away and tossed into the moat.

The four travellers went into the castle.

46

The old woman peered out of the slitted window at the flames below her. Smoke drifted in through the window, but neither the flames nor the roses reached the highest tower. She knew that the castle was being attacked, and she would have hidden in the tower room, had there been anywhere to hide, had the sleeper not been on the bed.

She swore, and began, laboriously, to walk down the steps, one at a time. She intended to make it down as far as the castle's battlements, from where she could reach the far side of the building, the cellars. She could hide there. She knew the building better than anybody. She was slow, but she was cunning, and she could wait. Oh, she could wait.

She heard their calls rising up the stairwell.

"This way!"

"Up here!"

"It feels worse this way. Come on! Quickly!"

She turned around, then, did her best to hurry upwards, but her legs moved no faster than they had when she was climbing earlier that day. They caught her just as she reached the top of the steps: three men, no higher than her hips, closely followed by a young woman in travel-stained clothes, with the blackest hair the old woman had ever seen.

47

The young woman said, "Seize her," in a tone of casual command.

The little men took her stick. "She's stronger than she looks," said one of them, his head still ringing from the blow she had got in with the stick, before he had taken it. They walked her back into the round tower room.

"The fire?" said the old woman, who had not talked to anyone who could answer her for six decades. "Was anyone killed in the fire? Did you see the king or the queen?"

The young woman shrugged. "I don't think so. The sleepers we passed were all inside, and the walls are thick. Who are you?"

Names. Names. The old woman squinted, then she shook her head. She was herself, and the name she had been born with had been eaten by time and lack of use.

"Where is the princess?"

The old woman just stared at her.

"And why are you awake?"

She said nothing. They spoke urgently to one another then, the little men and the queen. "Is she a witch? There's a magic about her, but I do not think it's of her making."

"Guard her," said the queen. "If she is a witch, that stick might be important. Keep it from her."

"It's my stick," said the old woman. "I think it was my father's. But he had no more use for it."

The queen ignored her. She walked to the bed, pulled down the silk netting. The sleeper's face stared blindly up at them.

"So this is where it began," said one of the little men.

"On her birthday," said another.

"Well," said the third. "Somebody's got to do the honours."

"I shall," said the queen, gently. She lowered her face to the sleeping woman's. She touched the pink lips to her own carmine lips and she kissed the sleeping girl long and hard.

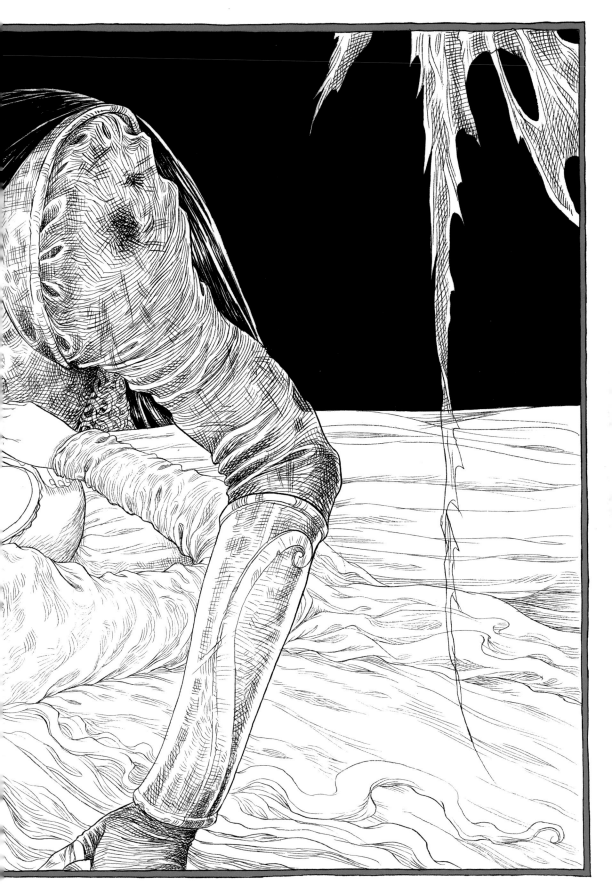

"Did it work?" asked a dwarf.

"I do not know," said the queen. "But I feel for her, poor thing. Sleeping her life away."

"You slept for a year in the same witch-sleep," said the dwarf. "You did not starve. You did not rot."

The figure on the bed stirred, as if she were having a bad dream from which she was fighting to wake herself.

The queen ignored her. She had noticed something on the floor beside the bed. She reached down and picked it up. "Now this," she said. "This smells of magic."

"There's magic all through this," said the smallest dwarf.

"No, *this*," said the queen. She showed him the wooden spindle, the base half wound around with yarn. "*This* smells of magic."

"It was here, in this room," said the old woman, suddenly. "And I was little more than a girl. I had never gone so far before, but I climbed all the steps, and I went up and up and round and round until I came to the topmost room. I saw that bed, the one you see, although there was nobody in it. There was only an old woman, sitting on the stool, spinning wool into yarn with her spindle. I had never seen a spindle before. She asked if I would like a go. She took the wool in her hand and gave me the spindle to hold. She held my thumb and pressed it against the point of the spindle until blood flowed, and she touched the blood to the thread. And then she said –"

Another voice interrupted her. A young voice it was, a girl's voice, but still sleep-thickened. "I said, now I take your sleep from you, girl, just as I take from you your ability to harm me in my sleep, for someone needs to be awake while I sleep. Your family, your friends, your world will sleep too. And then I lay down on the bed, and I slept, and they slept, and as each of them slept I stole a little of their life, a little of their dreams, and as I slept I took back my youth and my beauty and my power. I slept and I grew strong. I undid the ravages of time and I built myself a world of sleeping slaves."

She was sitting up in the bed. She looked so beautiful, and so very young.

The queen looked at the girl, and saw what she was searching for: the same look that she had seen in her stepmother's eyes, and she knew what manner of creature this girl was.

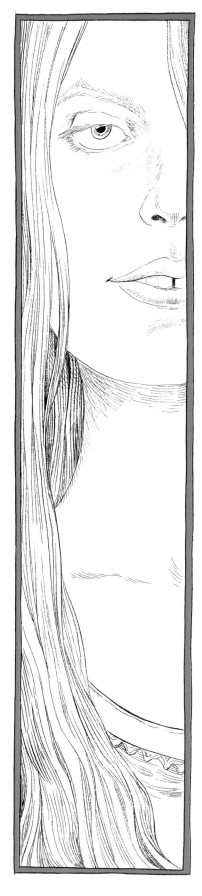

"We had been led to believe," said the tallest dwarf, "that when you woke, the rest of the world would wake with you."

"Why ever would you think that?" asked the golden-haired girl, all childlike and innocent (ah, but her eyes! Her eyes were so old). "I like them asleep. They are more . . . *biddable*." She stopped for a moment. Then she grinned. "Even now they come for you. I have called them here."

"It's a high tower," said the queen. "And sleeping people do not move fast. We still have a little time to talk, Your Darkness."

"Who are you? Why would we talk? Why do you know to address me that way?" The girl climbed off the bed and stretched deliciously, pushing each fingertip out before running her fingertips through her golden hair. She smiled, and it was as if the sun shone into that dim room. "The little people will stop where they are, now. I do not like them. And you, girl. You will sleep too."

"No," said the queen.

She hefted the spindle. The yarn wrapped around it was black with age and with time.

The dwarfs stopped where they stood, and they swayed, and closed their eyes.

The queen said, "It's always the same with your kind. You need youth and you need beauty. You used your own up so long ago, and now you find ever more complex ways of obtaining them. And you always want power."

They were almost nose to nose, now, and the fair-haired girl seemed so much younger than the queen.

"Why don't you just go to sleep?" asked the girl, and she smiled guilelessly, just as the queen's stepmother had smiled when she wanted something. There was a noise on the stairs, far below them.

"I slept for a year in a glass coffin," said the queen. "And the woman who put me there was much more powerful and dangerous than you will ever be."

"More powerful than I am?" The girl seemed amused. "I have a million sleepers under my control. With every

56

moment that I slept I grew in power, and the circle of dreams grows faster and faster with every passing day. I have my youth – so much youth! I have my beauty. No weapon can harm me. Nobody alive is more powerful than I am."

She stopped and stared at the queen.

"You are not of our blood," she said. "But you have some of the skill." She smiled, the smile of an innocent girl who has woken on a spring morning. "Ruling the world will not be easy. Nor will maintaining order among those of the Sisterhood who have survived into this degenerate age. I will need someone to be my eyes and ears, to administer justice, to attend to things when I am otherwise engaged. I will stay at the centre of the web. You will not rule with me, but beneath me, but you will still rule, and rule continents, not just a tiny kingdom." She reached out a hand and stroked the queen's pale skin, which, in the dim light of that room, seemed almost as white as snow.

The queen said nothing.

"Love me," said the girl. "All will love me, and you, who woke me, you must love me most of all."

The queen felt something stirring in her heart. She remembered her stepmother, then. Her stepmother had liked to be adored. Learning how to be strong, to feel her own emotions and not another's, had been hard; but once you learned the trick of it, you did not forget. And she did not wish to rule continents.

The girl smiled at her with eyes the colour of the morning sky.

The queen did not smile. She reached out her hand. "Here," she said. "This is not mine."

She passed the spindle to the old woman beside her. The old woman hefted it, thoughtfully. She began to unwrap the yarn from the spindle with arthritic fingers. "This was my life," she said. "This thread was my life . . ."

"It *was* your life. You gave it to me," said the sleeper, irritably. "And it has gone on much too long."

The tip of the spindle was still sharp after so many decades.

The old woman, who had once been a princess, held the yarn tightly in her hand, and she thrust the point of the spindle into the golden-haired girl's breast.

The girl watched as a trickle of red blood ran down her breast and stained her white dress crimson.

"No weapon can harm me," she said, and her girlish voice was petulant. "Not any more. Look. It's only a scratch."

"It's not a weapon," said the queen. "It's your own magic. And a scratch is all that was needed."

The girl's blood soaked into the thread that had once been wrapped about the spindle, the thread that ran from the spindle to the raw wool in the old woman's hand.

The girl looked down at the blood staining her dress, and at the blood on the thread, and she said only, "It was just a prick of the skin, nothing more." She seemed confused.

The noise on the stairs was getting louder. A slow, irregular shuffling, as if a hundred sleepwalkers were coming up a stone spiral staircase with their eyes closed.

The room was small, and there was nowhere to hide, and the room's windows were two narrow slits in the stones.

The old woman, who had not slept in so many decades, said, "You took my dreams. You took my sleep. Now, that's enough of all that." She was a very old woman. Her fingers were gnarled, like the roots of a hawthorn bush. Her nose was long, and her eyelids drooped, but there was a look in her eyes in that moment that was the look of someone young.

She swayed, and then she staggered, and she would have fallen to the floor if the queen had not caught her first.

The queen carried the old woman to the bed, marvelling at how little she weighed, and

62

placed her on the crimson counterpane. The old woman's chest rose and fell.

The noise on the stairs was louder now. Then a silence, followed suddenly by a hubbub, as if a hundred people were talking at once, surprised and angry and confused.

The beautiful girl said, "But —" and now there was nothing girlish or beautiful about her. Her face fell and became less shapely. She reached down to the smallest dwarf, pulled his hand-axe from his belt. She fumbled with the axe, held it up threateningly, with hands all wrinkled and worn.

The queen drew her sword (the blade's edge was notched and damaged from the thorns), but instead of striking, she took a step backwards.

"Listen! They are waking up," she said. "They are all waking up. Tell me again about the youth you stole from them. Tell me again about your beauty and your power. Tell me again how clever you were, Your Darkness."

When the people reached the tower room, they saw an old woman asleep on a bed, and they saw the queen, standing tall, and beside her, the dwarfs, who were shaking their heads, or scratching them.

They saw something else on the floor also: a tumble of bones, a hank of hair as fine and as white as fresh-spun cobwebs, a tracery of grey rags across it, and over all of it, an oily dust.

"Take care of her," said the queen, pointing with the dark wooden spindle at the old woman on the bed. "She saved your lives."

She left, then, with the dwarfs. None of the people in that room or on the steps dared to stop them or would ever understand what had happened.

A mile or so from the castle, in a clearing in the Forest of Acaire, the queen and the dwarfs lit a fire of dry twigs, and in it they burned the thread and the fibre. The smallest dwarf chopped the spindle into fragments of black wood with his axe, and they burned them too. The wood chips gave off a noxious smoke as they burned, which made the queen cough, and the smell of old magic was heavy in the air.

Afterwards, they buried the charred wooden fragments beneath a rowan tree.

By evening they were on the outskirts of the forest, and had reached a cleared track. They could see a village across the hill, and smoke rising from the village chimneys.

"So," said the dwarf with the brown beard. "If we head due west, we can be at the mountains by the end of the week, and we'll have you back in your palace in Kanselaire within ten days."

"Yes," said the queen.

"And your wedding will be late, but it will happen soon after your return, and the people will celebrate, and there will be joy unbounded through the kingdom."

"Yes," said the queen. She said nothing, but sat on the moss beneath an oak tree and tasted the stillness, heartbeat by heartbeat.

There are choices, she thought, when she had sat long enough. *There are always choices.*

She made one.

The queen began to walk, and the dwarfs followed her.

"You *do* know we're heading east, don't you?" said one of the dwarfs.

"Oh yes," said the queen.

"Well, *that's* all right then," said the dwarf.

They walked to the east, all four of them, away from the sunset and the lands they knew, and into the night.

They walked to the
east,
all four of them, away
from the sunset and
the lands they knew,
and
into
the
Night.

BOOKS BY NEIL GAIMAN FROM BLOOMSBURY

NOVELS

Illustrated by Chris Riddell
Fortunately, the Milk . . .
The Graveyard Book
Coraline

Odd and the Frost Giants

SHORT STORIES

M is for Magic

PICTURE BOOKS

Illustrated by Dave McKean
Crazy Hair
The Day I Swapped My Dad for Two Goldfish
The Wolves in the Walls

Illustrated by Charles Vess
Instructions
Blueberry Girl

Illustrated by Gris Grimly
The Dangerous Alphabet

Illustrated by Adam Rex
Chu's Day
Chu's First Day at School

GRAPHIC NOVELS

Illustrated by Dave McKean
Signal to Noise
The Tragical Comedy or Comical Tragedy of Mr Punch
MirrorMask

Illustrated by P. Craig Russell
Coraline
The Graveyard Book: Volume One
The Graveyard Book: Volume Two